Hello Rameses!

Livy—
It was a
little hand for
me to send you
this book! I hope
you like it!
Love you.
Aunt Lise

Aimee Aryal

Illustrated by Blair Cooper

It was a beautiful fall day at the
University of North Carolina.

Rameses was on his way to the
Dean E. Smith Center to watch
a basketball game.

He passed in front of South Building
and walked down Polk Place.

A professor walking by said,
"Hello Rameses!"

Rameses stopped at Davis Library.

A librarian who works inside waved,
"Hello Rameses!"

Rameses went to The Pit
near the Student Union.

Some students studying there said,
"Hello Rameses!"

Rameses walked by
Morehead-Patterson Bell Tower.

A couple who stopped to listen to the
bells waved, "Hello Rameses!"

Rameses walked past Kenan Stadium
where the Tar Heels play football.

Some UNC fans standing nearby said,
"Hello Rameses!"

As Rameses walked to the Smith Center,
he passed by some alumni.

The alumni remembered Rameses
from when they went to UNC.
They said, "Hello, again, Rameses!"

Finally, Rameses arrived at the
"Dean Dome."

As he ran onto the basketball court,
the crowd cheered,
"Let's Go Tar Heels!"

Rameses watched the game from
the sidelines and cheered
for the team.

The Tar Heels scored a basket!
The players shouted,
"Slam Dunk Rameses!"

The UNC Tar Heels won the game!

Rameses gave Coach Williams
a high-five. The coach said,
"Great game Rameses!"

After the basketball game, Rameses
was tired. It had been a long day at
the University of North Carolina.

He walked home and climbed into bed.

"Goodnight Rameses."

For Anna and Maya,
and all of Rameses' little fans. ~ AA

For Lauren Woodruff. ~ BC

Special thanks to:

Carolyn Elfland

Courtney Deadmon Weller

Roy Williams

For information please contact Mascot Books,
P.O. Box 220157, Chantilly, VA 20153-0157.

UNIVERSITY OF NORTH CAROLINA, TAR HEELS, UNC, NORTH CAROLINA and CAROLINA
are trademarks or registered trademarks of the University of North Carolina
and are used under license.

ISBN: 1-932888-17-9

Printed in the United States.

www.mascotbooks.com